I Made A Mistake

I Made A Mistake

based on a jump rope rhyme

Written and Illustrated by
MIRIAM NERLOVE

A Margaret K. McElderry Book
Atheneum   1985   New York

All of the material contained herein is original
with the exception of the second and tenth couplets.

Library of Congress Cataloging in Publication Data

Nerlove, Miriam.
I made a mistake.

"A Margaret K. McElderry book."
Summary: A little girl's blunderings surprise a
number of animals.
1. Jump rope rhymes.   2. Children's poetry, American.
[1. Jump rope rhymes.   2. American poetry]   I. Title.
PS3564.E65I2 1985   811'.54   85-6018
ISBN 0-689-50327-X

Copyright © 1985 by Miriam Nerlove
Published simultaneously in Canada by McClelland & Stewart Ltd.
Composition by Dix Type, Syracuse, New York
Printed by Connecticut Printers
Bound by Halliday Lithograph Corporation
Typography by Christine Kettner
First edition

To my grandmother

I went to the bathroom to brush my hair,
I made a mistake . . .

and brushed a bear.

I went to the kitchen to bake a pie,
I made a mistake . . .

and baked a fly.

I went to the pantry to look for some jam,
I made a mistake . . .

and discovered a lamb.

I went outside to sit on the lawn,
I made a mistake . . .

and sat on a swan.

I went to the park to walk the dog,
I made a mistake . . .

and walked a frog.

I went through my drawers to find a blouse,
I made a mistake . . .

and found a mouse.

I went to the well to make a wish,
I made a mistake . . .

and kissed a fish.

I went to the laundry to wash my socks,
I made a mistake . . .

and washed a fox.

I went to the sea to go for a sail,
I made a mistake . . .

and rode on a whale.

I went to the barn to milk the cow,
I made a mistake . . .

and milked a sow.

I went to the store to buy a cake,
I made a mistake . . .

and bought a snake.

I went to the closet to put on my hat,
I made a mistake . . .

and put on the cat.

I went next door to find my friend,
I made a mistake . . .

and found THE END.